'Get well quickly!'
Love from your
Aunt Mary
October 1983

TREASURE ISLAND

TREASURE ISLAND

R. L. Stevenson

Illustrated by Jack Matthew

BLACKIE: LONDON AND GLASGOW

ISBN 0 216 88508 6

Blackie & Son Limited
A Member of the Blackie Group
450 Edgware Road,
London W2 1EG

Distributed in the United States by
Two Continents Publishing Group Ltd.,
30 East 42nd Street, New York, NY 10017

Printed in Great Britain